Sylvanhome

Sylvanhome

by Douglas Sun

www.ramensandwich.com

FIRST EDITION

Library of Congress Cataloging-in-Publication Data: Sun,

Douglas
Sylvanhome / by Douglas Sun
– 1st ed. ISBN 978-0-9970793-6-4
1.   Gaming – Dungeons and Dragons. 2.Gaming
– roleplaying 3. Sci-Fi and Fantasy – Teens
I.   Sun, Douglas II. Sylvanhome

Places by the Way is dedicated
to all dungeon masters and heroic
adventurers of every generation,
regardless of which edition of
Dungeons & Dragons you favor.

Keep your blade sharp and your
spellbook handy; and may you always
have a natural 20 in your pocket for
your moment of direst need.

-Douglas Sun

CONTENTS

Chapter One

Chapter Two

Chapter Three

Chapter Four

Encounter Tables

NPC's and Creatures

Errata

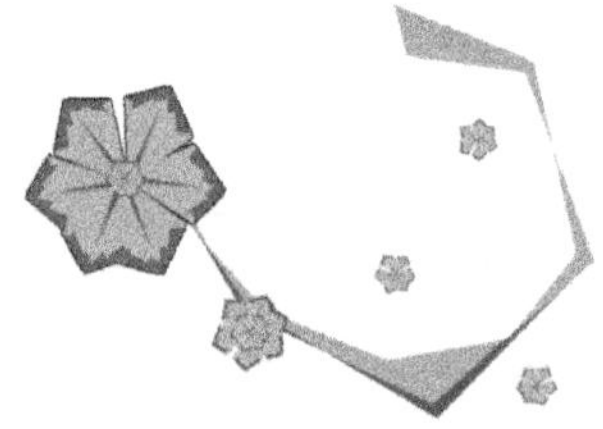

INTRODUCTION

Sylvanhome is the fourth in our **Places by the Way** series of location modules. Places by the Way will offer you an assortment of colorful pieces to help you fill out your campaign world. Even the most epic campaigns need interludes — places where heroes can regroup and pursue amusing side quests in between world-saving feats of derring-do.

Think of **Places by the Way** as kits for such interludes.

The fate of your entire campaign world need not turn on anything that is described in these pages. But even so, the heroes in your campaign will need to refill their empty quivers and packs; buy tools and potions; upgrade their arms and armor. Or they need a safe place to lay up for the night, untroubled by beasts of the wild, so they can heal and recover spells. Every campaign needs changes of pace to make the epic moments seem bigger. We can help you make those changes of pace engaging.

We understand that adventure can still be had in places found by the way.

Sylvanhome is compatible with the Dungeons & Dragons 5th Edition rules and assumes that you have access to the core rule books. It is not set in any particular campaign world, and we hope that you will find it compatible with your own world with only a bit of patching. We have published a parallel module, *Elves of Semberholme*, set in the Forgotten Realms. It is also compatible with the Dungeons & Dragons 5th Edition rules.

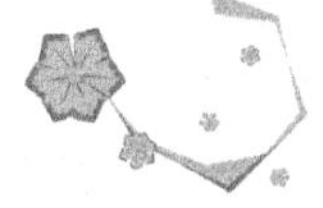

HOW TO USE THIS BOOK

Sylvanhome describes a community of wood elves who live nestled in a corner of the forest that has been inhabited by elves for at least as long as anyone can remember. It is an isolated place — but not so deep and hidden that a band of humans making their living as hunters and woodsmen couldn't stumble upon them, as happened not too long ago. These humans originated from settlements outside the forest, but they have set up a camp only a few miles from Sylvanhome and it is clear to the elves that they aren't going away anytime soon.

Chance encounters between foraging parties from both communities were the first, uneasy contacts between the humans and elves. Since then, the elder of Sylvanhome, Guillen Longsea (see location #3) has met with representatives of the humans to discuss sharing the lands around Sylvanhome. The communities have even exchanged high-ranking hostages to ensure each other's good conduct. However, the elves and the humans have not yet made any lasting agreements with each other, and both sides seem to be marking time, as if waiting for something to move them to action one way or another. Occasional incursions by human criminals looking for a refuge from justice have done nothing to increase the level of trust between the elves and the humans, as the long-isolated elves don't have the experience to make subtle distinctions among alien races — in short, all humans look alike to them.

The wood elves' own basic nature lies close to the heart of the problem. Humans are prone to take for themselves whatever they find, and they're always looking for new territory — that is their basic nature. But wood elves prefer to keep to themselves and guard what is theirs jealously, and they instinctively suspect the intentions of anyone who is not part of their in-group. Like their more "civilized" cousins the high elves, wood elves think of themselves as bearing good will toward all beings, but at the same time they are quick to treat any non-elf who is not already known to them as a potential threat.

This division in their essential nature defines how the wood elves of Sylvanhome feel about their new neighbors at this time. There is a faction in the village, led by Ilwen Sylla (see location #4) who sees no malice in the humans next door and would like to work out some form of peaceful coexistence with them, sharing access to this corner of the forest and its resources.

But there is another faction, many of them influenced by the bard Lucan Bellfae (see location #5) who resent humans encroaching on elven land. They fear that the humans intend to overwhelm the elves of Sylvanhome and drive them out — whether quickly by force or over time by sheer weight of numbers (given their higher birth rate and knack for migration), it does not matter. The end result will be the same. Lucan's faction argues that Sylvanhome has no reasonable option but to push back against the humans — at least, stop them from encroaching any further into the forest, and driving them back into the plains if possible.

However, most of Sylvanhome's elves aren't sure whether they agree with one side or the other. They don't know what to make of the humans, and more than anything else they're waiting to see how things play out. Sylvanhome's leader falls into this category, precisely because the weight of opinion in Sylvanhome could shift heavily one way or the other depending on what happens going forward. The future of the village would seem to rest on a precarious balance, and your party has the chance to tip it one way or another depending on their actions.

Chapter 1 freezes the community of Sylvanhome at a moment in time. It preserves a slice of its collective life and describes what the party sees and experiences on a casual visit. Use as much or as little of this chapter as you like. But if you want to use any of the material in Chapters 2-4, then going through the material in Chapter 1 should provide your party with at least a hook or two that leads them into those plot lines.

Chapters 2-4 describe subplots that you can offer the party at your discretion, and that they can accept or refuse at their discretion. They need not be presented and resolved in any particular order, although Chapter 2 and Chapter 4 offer natural points of conclusion for the party's involvement with Sylvanhome.

In Chapter 2, Lucan the bard tries to gull the party into kidnapping Caerwen Sylla and returning him to Sylvanhome, thus destroying the hostage exchange between the village and the hunters and crippling diplomacy between the elves and the humans. This Chapter gives the party the chance to do something that creates real problems for Sylvanhome, and if they succeed they'll return to the village and find it in a tense situation that will only become more difficult and complicated over time. So feel free to skip over it if you wish.

In Chapter 3, the party gets the chance to rescue Uwel the scout (see location #10) after he falls into the hands of bandits from whom he has stolen a valuable item.

Chapter 4 becomes available to the party if they meet certain preconditions (none of them are unlikely or particularly onerous). Commander of the village sentries Ilwen Sylla asks for the party's help as she and one of the human leaders agree to join forces to hunt down a werewolf who caused the death of a hunter. If the mission succeeds, it could mark a turning point in relations between the two communities, as it would mark the first time they allied to face a common threat.

Sylvanhome assumes a baseline of a party of 4-6 characters with an average level of 1-3, but it does not require a party of any particular size or level. Where it makes sense to do so, the encounters are scaled according to the party's average level, assuming a standard party of 4-6 characters,

Treat all NPCs as commoners unless otherwise noted, In which case their stats are listed at the end, under NPC Stat Blocks. All elvish commoners should have elvish racial abilities, of course. Also, note that the residents of Sylvanhome have very little coin compared to most communities; since they don't trade with other communities and they feel comfortable bartering amongst themselves, they have never seen much need for it. Many families have semiprecious gems or jewelry of modest value as keepsakes or heirlooms, but to have coins on hand worth more than 20 gp total would be unusual. However, every household keeps a longbow and a quiver of 20 arrows handy for when a member must do militia service (see location #1). Most also have a coil of spider silk rope (see location #9) between 50 and 100 feet in length, depending on how far they need to climb between the ground and their residence.

SETTING THE SCENE

How and why the party has come to the forest does not matter. Perhaps they are looking for a shortcut, gambling that going straight through the forest will cost them less time than going around it. Perhaps they have heard the object of their quest lies hidden among the trees. Perhaps the half-orc barbarian had to relieve himself and got lost. Any reason will do.

The forest seems like it goes on forever — mostly because the density of the foliage prevents you from seeing very far. Perhaps you hear a nearby stream murmuring, the distant chirp of birdsong or noises of insects and small animals. But other than that, the silence of the deep forest is palpable. If you pause and let your senses take over, you realize that you can actually hear the quiet.

At some point, you realize that the trees are thinning out a bit, but each tree is larger and its branches spread out more broadly than the ones you have just passed. If you concentrate on the far distance, you can see in the thick branches of distant trees wooden structures half-hidden among the leaves. You glimpse slight, slender figures moving around on the ground and up and down from the trees, rappelling or using ladders. They move so gracefully that they seem visible one moment and invisible the next, all the more so as their copper-colored skin and the earth tones of their garb meld with the natural colors of the forest. If they see you, they look out of the corner of an eye, or peek from behind a tree. Then they return to their business. A thought emerges from a corner of your mind that they would rather that you go away and leave them alone.

The party has reached the village of Sylvanhome, in lands inhabited since time immemorial by the elves of the woods. Are they welcome here? That remains to be seen.

Chapter 1: Sylvanhome

Random Encounters – The Forest

Sylvanhome has maintained its isolation for so long in large part because it is surrounded by wilderness. However, that is not to say that the forest is empty. If the party spends considerable time in the surrounding forest, you may throw a random encounter at them. Roll on Table 1.1, or just select one that you prefer.

Table 1.1: Random Encounters

d20	Encounter
1-3	Wolves
4-6	Spider lair
7-8	Hunting party
9-10	Uwel at work
11-12	Bandit scout
13-14	Wererat
15-16	Brown bear
17-18	Giant badger
19-20	Ranger Smith

Wolves. The party hears canine snarling from the shadows of the trees. A pack of 4-6 wolves confronts them. If you wish to scale up the encounter, use dire wolves if the average level of the party is 4 or higher.

Spider lair. A giant spider has anchored its web on the trunk and lowest branches of a dead tree.

If the average level of the party is 4-6, there are two giant spiders.

If the average level of the party is 7-9, there are three giant spiders.

If the average level of the party is 10 or higher, there are five giant spiders.

Treasure: There are 10-20 gp and 50-70 sp scattered around the web.

Hunting party. The party encounters three hunters from the human camp. They greet the party casually and don't bother to put their guard up. If the party reveals that they have come from Sylvanhome, the hunters treat this as a matter of fact and don't show much reaction — except, perhaps, that the foremost among them asks about the welfare of Fairley Rehn, their hostage in the elven village (see location #8):

"His mother and father surely miss him, but they understand how it is. Until we can work something out with those elves, I reckon this is how it's going to have to be.

"Well, you can tell them that that elven boy come to live with us is having himself a fine time. He's always asking us about our ways, our history. He's even learning our songs and stories. I guess everyone likes him well enough, although he kind of makes folk nervous when he looks over their shoulders at what they're doing."

Treat one of the hunters as a scout and the other two as commoners with longbows.

Uwel at work. If it is night, the party may come upon Uwel the scout patrolling the forest surrounding Sylvanhome (see location #10). If you wish to convey information to the party about elements of your campaign that occur within the forest, but fall outside the scope of this module, Uwel may introduce it for you in the course of making conversation.

Bandit scout. A bandit from the gang based at location #14 scouts the surrounding forest. He tries to hide and observe the party. If they spot him, he flees. If they capture and interrogate him, a successful DC 15 Charisma (Intimidation) check gets him to reveal the existence of the gang, their numbers and something of their organizational structure.

Wererat. Unbeknownst to just about everyone at this point, lycanthropy has spread into the forest near Sylvanhome. The party gets a foretaste when it comes upon a wererat in its humanoid form. It tries to convince the party that it is a woodsman from the hunting camp. If the party turns its back on the wererat it polymorphs into its hybrid form and attacks.

If the party has no magic or silvered weapons, you may want to hold off on throwing a lycanthrope at them.

If the party's average level is 10 or higher, they encounter two wererats.

Brown bear. It's a forest. There are bears here. They aren't aggressive. If confronted, they rear up on their hind legs and roar to try to scare off the party. They do not fight unless attacked. If you do want to set up a battle, one brown bear is a modest challenge for a party with an average level of 1-3.

If the average level of the party is 4-6, there are two brown bears.

If the average level of the party is 7-9, there are three brown bears

If the average level of the party is 10 or higher, there are five brown bears.

Giant badgers. Two giant badgers snarl at the party from inside a hollow tree trunk. If the party approaches within 10 feet of the trunk, the badgers attack.

1. Guard Posts

If you approach Sylvanhome from any angle (except burrowing from underground) you're being watched, whether you realize it or not. Six strategically placed guard posts ring the village and allow discreet observation of all approaches.

Each post consists of a 5' x 5' wooden platform wedged about 20 feet up in a tall tree and concealed among the branches. A lone sentry mans each post at all times, wearing leather armor covered in leaves and equipped with a longbow. Since elves don't get particularly sleepy, sentries work a half-day shift and their vigilance never lapses. Use of camouflage and natural concealment makes them hard to spot from the ground — this requires a successful DC 18 Wisdom (Perception) check if the sentry is trying to remain hidden, and a DC 10 Wisdom (Perception) check even if the sentry is not trying to conceal himself. In combat, they get partial cover as long as they remain on the platform.

Therefore, a party approaching the outskirts of Sylvanhome hears a voice out of nowhere ordering them to halt and state their business. The sight of an arrow fitted to a longbow and pointing at the party from out of rustling leaves soon follows. If the party presents proof that it has legitimate business in the village, or if it contains at least one elf character who steps forward and vouches for the group, then the sentry lets them pass.

If the party has nothing obvious to mark it as harmless, getting a pass is more difficult. You may allow one character to speak for the party and insist on a DC 15 Charisma (Persuasion) to sway the sentry. Or you may cut to the chase and have the sentry blow a loud, high whistle to draw the attention of the garrison commander, Ilwen Sylla (see location #4). Within minutes, she arrives on scene, flanked by four of the off-duty sentries, and she decides whether to allow the party to enter the village.

Treasure: None of the guard posts contain any treasure.

Scaling the Encounter: Treat the sentries as guards with longbows and elven racial abilities. Treat Sylla as a 3rd Level ranger (see NPC stat blocks).

2. Speaker's Clearing

This small clearing is Sylvanhome's equivalent of a town square. It's barely large enough to fit all of the adult villagers and whenever a matter requires general discussion or the elder wishes to make an announcement, everyone gathers here. Communal worship of the deity of the elves also takes place here.

By informal agreement with the elder, Lucan the bard (see location #5) also uses it as his place of business. Every late afternoon and evening, Lucan serves up his distinctive liquor here and regales his customers with traditional elven songs. Some folks come for the booze, some come for the music and others still take equal pleasure in both. They'll stay until the modest supply of adult beverages runs out. During that time the party may pick up bits of news and gossip about Sylvanhome and the surrounding area, and if it suits your campaign, its relationship to the wider world. Sylvanhome is an isolated community, but the appearance of the human hunters in the neighborhood also means that it has come into contact with the wider world — and in fact, that qualified isolation could distort the importance of whatever information from the outside world you want to filter through it to your players. Whatever it is, it can seem more alarming because the locals don't know enough to put it into context, or they can minimize it for exactly the same reason. If you're looking to test your party's ability to separate fact from fiction, this setting gives you the opportunity.

3. Elder's Residence/Village Shrine

This complex of rooms fills the branches of a large tree at the center of Sylvanhome. The elder of the village lives here, and it also serves as the main shrine to Sylvanhome's divine patron, the deity of the elves.

However, communal worship does not take place here; there isn't a room large enough to accommodate everyone who would take part. Instead, the *Idol of Sylvanhome* (see New Magic Item), which is carved from rare and unusually hard wood of indeterminate origin in a stylized representation of the elven deity's holy symbol, sits on a pedestal in a small room, where the elder communes with the divine by meditating in its presence during his rest hours. For communal worship, it is secured by a spider silk rope such as the ones made by Aela and Luven Welleaf (see location #9), lowered to the ground and carried into the speaker's clearing (see location #2).

The current elder is Guillen Longsea, a heavy-set (by elven standards) fellow whose large eyes and reedy voice make him seem younger than he is in reality. He inherited the position from his mother, a grey elf named Elna who decided to retire and who now lives in a small house on the outskirts of the village (see location #12). Guillen does the best he can to lead and administer Sylvanhome and he has gained the tentative respect of its residents. But his venerable mother casts her shadow, try as she does to let to her son govern in his own right. In all of his dealings with his fellow villagers, he senses in their gaze a question: "What would the Lady Elna do in his place?"

This insecurity informs his actions and decisions regarding the neighboring humans. He knows no better than anyone else what to make of them, whether they're friends of enemies. He is open to arguments either way, and it's not hard for Ilwen Sylla and Lucan the bard to pull him one way and then the other. The net result is that under his leadership, Sylvanhome sits on its hands and waits for what the future will bring them.

Treat Guillen Longsea as a 2nd level cleric (see NPC stat blocks).

Treasure: The idol of the elven deity has little material value — no precious gems or inlaid metals — but based on its rarity and workmanship, a collector might pay 800 gp for this exotic artifact of the wood elves. Without the elder of Sylvanhome to activate it, it has no magical properties outside of the village; it's just an art object.

A locked closet holds the village treasury in loosely tied sacks: 58 pp, 300 gp and 12 gems worth 1,000 gp all together. Guillen keeps the key on his person at all times, but otherwise picking the lock requires a successful DC 15 Dexterity (Sleight of Hand) check.

4. Ilwen Sylla's Headquarters

Sylvanhome is not a militarized society. The sentries are ordinary members of the community who take turns at serving guard duty, making themselves available every day for a full year, and at the end of that term they return to private life. In other words, they're more like a militia than a professional military. The only permanent member of the garrison is its leader, Ilwen Sylla.

This constellation of rooms set amongst the branches of a large tree serve as Ilwen's residence and the garrison's headquarters. The six off-duty sentries can be found here at all times, either resting in a private room or relaxing in the large common area. They are Ilwen's emergency response team and they stand ready to respond in case one of the guard posts reports an emergency.

Ilwen Sylla cuts an imposing figure when you first meet her. She is tall and broad-shouldered for an elf, and her narrow eyes convey the feeling that she is always scrutinizing you. She is a ranger by trade, and she served the village as a scout patrolling the surrounding forest (the role that Uwel — see location #10 — now fills) before being promoted to garrison leader.

However, her appearance belies her peaceful nature. In the debate over how to deal with Sylvanhome's human neighbors, Ilwen comes down firmly on the side of cooperation and forbearance (at least, with regard to humans who are not openly hostile to elves). She is always at loggerheads with Lucan (see location #5) when this subject comes up for discussion.

Friendly disposition toward humans runs in her family. Her fraternal twin brother Caerwen Sylla currently lives with the neighboring humans as Sylvanhome's part of a hostage exchange meant to safeguard peaceful relations between the two communities (see location #8). While Caerwen didn't really volunteer for it, neither did he go unwillingly. Once Guillen Longsea made the deal, Caerwen and Ilwen discussed it with the elder and all agreed that their village should send a hostage who favored peaceful coexistence. If the elder were to select an unwilling hostage, it would give Lucan and those who follow his way of thinking leverage if they chose to argue that peace with the humans was hurting the community. Although she has not heard from her brother in some time, Ilwen continues to stand by their decision, even as she lives with the knowledge that her brother is not so much a hostage to the humans as to possible events that could spin out of anyone's ability to control them.

Treasure: Ilwen Sylla has little personal wealth of her own. In a small locked chest in her bedroom — successful DC 15 Dexterity (Sleight of Hand) check to open — she keeps 50 gp, 300 sp and an heirloom silver brooch with an emerald set in it worth 200 gp. In her office there is a locked chest — also a successful DC 15 Dexterity (Sleight of Hand) check to open — with 1,000 sp in it; this represents the garrison's budget.

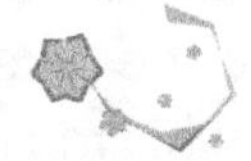

5. Lucan the Bard

Lucan Bellfae occupies a complication position in Sylvanhome. On the one hand, he keeps the community entertained with his musical and dramatic talents, and he keeps them lubricated with alcoholic beverages that he distills himself. This makes him popular. But he also stridently opposes the presence of humans in this corner of the forest, and not all of his fellow residents agree with him on that score. He believes that Sylvanhome and the surrounding area belongs to the elves alone, since elves have lived there since time immemorial, and everyone else should leave — by force, if necessary.

Lucan's role as the village bard gives him a bully pulpit for his beliefs, but he takes care to refrain from preaching through his music. Instead, he chooses his repertoire carefully from traditional elven songs, and the more ancient the better. His sad songs tend toward tales of lands once held by the elves, but since lost to other races (mostly evil humanoids, as everyone agrees about hating orcs and the like), and forbidden love between elves and non-elves that turned out badly. His upbeat songs often celebrate the glories of elven culture and past feats of elven arms. Subtly, his chosen catalogue of songs sends the message that non-elves mean trouble, but that when elves stand up for themselves, they triumph over their enemies.

As a performer, Lucan is popular in Sylvanhome because he is such a talented musician that he can make almost anything sound good. But many songs in his repertoire tell of lands so far and away and events so long ago that many find them obscure. In truth, Lucan inherited his vast knowledge of traditional elven song from his high-elven father, who emigrated to Sylvahnhome. Lucan's father always saw the wood elves of his adopted home as ignorant and uncivilized, and Lucan himself inherited something of this snobbery. He won't come out and say it, but he believes deep down that wood elves don't necessarily know what's good for them, but maybe they would if they were properly exposed to the elven high culture that he learned from his father.

In public debates, Lucan has little patience with Ilwen Sylla and those who agree with her. He always argues that the humans are not to be trusted, regardless that the hunters have given one of their own as a hostage (see location #8). He always keeps a close eye on the elder to judge how the wind is blowing with him. If Lucan is concerned that the Guillen

Longsea is leaning too far toward cooperation with the humans, he demands a private audience and harangues him about the threat that they supposedly constitute.

On the ground, next to Lucan's tree, he maintains a small hut that contains the still in which he brews liquor from fruits and and pinecones gathered from the surrounding forest. His recipes are also part of his high-elven inheritance, modified slightly to fit local ingredients. As a result, Lucan's liquors are unique, as well as potent and flavorful, and they would probably command a high price in the world outside of the forest.

If the party converses with Lucan, he takes a little time to size them up, then offers them a proposition:

The bard smiles at you, his eyes narrow and a corner of his mouth turns up. "Perhaps you can help me," he says, his voice tuned to its silkiest timbre. There is a fruit that I use in some of my creations that we elves call the greenstone, on account of its pit. I usually get them from Lio the merchant, but lately he hasn't had any for me. I'd ask Uwel to look for some — but between you and me, I wouldn't rely on him to find his own boots in the morning, if you catch my meaning. But you look reliable. I'll reward you if you can find some for me."

If the party agrees, Lucan gives them a description of the fruit and its tree, some directions to a spot in the forest where they grow, and an empty basket. His directions are a little vague, but anyone with a bit of woodcraft or competence following directions should find the greenstone trees. A character who makes a successful DC 12 Wisdom (Survival) or Wisdom (Insight) check finds them easily enough. If no characters succeed, then the party wanders around in circles for a bit and is subject to a random encounter of your choice (see Table 1.1).

If the party returns to Lucan with a basket full of greenstone, he gives them 20 gp and a small bottle with five shots of one of his liquors. This unique concoction would probably fetch 100 gp in the outside world based on its rarity. One shot gives the imbiber a +1 bonus to all Strength saves and a +2 bonus to Strength-related skill checks, and a -1 penalty to Wisdom saves and a -2 penalty to Wisdom-related skill checks for four hours.

This quest, while it has some value in and of itself, is a test on Lucan's part, to see if he can trust the party with other requests later on.

Treat Lucan as a 5th level bard (see NPC stat blocks).

Treasure: Lucan is wealthy by Sylvanhome's standards, and much of it is inherited wealth. He keeps 1,146 gp, 251 sp and 15 gemstones worth 2,000 gp in a small chest in his bedroom.

6. Lin the Fletcher

Crafting arrows runs in Lin Gellwyn's family; he comes from a long line of fletchers. Having absorbed the expertise of his forbears, he has the skill to fashion projectiles that are remarkably true in flight and potent in their penetrating power. Close examination of his arrows reveal little out of the ordinary except perhaps for small barbs on the head that cause some extra shredding once the point has penetrated the target. But all of Lin's arrows should be treated as *+1 arrows* except that they are not magical.

The largest room in Lin's house is his workshop. Shavings, stripped bark and tools clutter the center of the room, and piles of branches and loose arrowheads lie about at the edges. Lin meets potential customers in this room, but there is no place for visitors to sit, and he does not offer to create one.

Even by elven standards, Lin is a slender and wiry fellow. He has thinning pale hair and his face never really uncurls from an aggravated stare. The party shouldn't take it personally if he seems unfriendly; that's just how he looks, and if he comes off as curt, that's how he treats all outsiders. Even elves from other villages would find him a little off-putting.

True to his nature, Lin barters freely with other Sylvanhome residents for his arrows, but he doesn't like selling them to non-elves. He swears that he'll never share them with the nearby humans; he won't do anything that encourages them to stay in the neighborhood. He'll sell them to the party, but only if the price is right — up to 20 arrows at 5 gp each. An elven character may bargain him down to 3 gp each with a successful DC 20 Charisma (Persuasion) test. A non-elven character may do the same, but at a disadvantage.

Treasure: Lin keeps no coin on hand. He wears a silver pendant with an emerald — a family heirloom worth 250 gp. He keeps his current supply of his handiwork — at the moment, 58 arrows, but this ebbs and flows in the normal course of business — in a barrel in one corner of his workshop.

7. Lio's General Store

Lio Welleaf runs Sylvanhome's general store. It's a small establishment and because wood elves tend to be homogenous in their tastes and needs, he doesn't need to keep a wide variety of goods. Even so, just about every basic item listed in the *Players Handbook* can be purchased here.

The store's featured product is a food staple that the local elves call forest bread. There is no agriculture in and around Sylvanhome. Instead of grains, they use nuts and seeds and stir them into a mash made from plants gathered from the forest floor that serves as a binding agent. Then they dry and lightly bake the mixture. Different elven villages have different recipes, based on the local selection of wild plants. But the universal end result is that forest bread is twice as filling as normal traveler's rations. In other words, 1/2 pound of forest bread would fully feed a character for one day. Also, a character who consumes 1/2 pound of forest bread in one day doubles his Constitution bonus for the purpose of saving throws made to determine state of exhaustion during the following day.

A successful DC 12 Charisma (Persuasion) check

convinces Lio to sell forest bread to non-elves. His price is 5 gp per pound, and he will not back off of it.

Lio also sells spider silk rope made by his niece Aela (see location #9) for 50 gp per 50-foot length. He will not back off of that price, either.

Treasure: Lio Welleaf keeps a small cashbox with 50 sp and 10 gp in it behind the counter. He insists on cash payment from outsiders, but he is always willing to barter with fellow elves. Hence, he has less cash on hand than a typical establishment of this type.

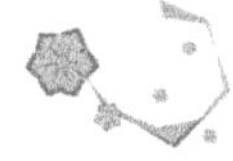

8. Fairley the Human

Fairley Rehn is a strong-willed human teenaged lad
whose family holds influence among the hunters who
venture into forest near Sylvanhome. Elves and their
ways have fascinated him since he was a child from
hearing folk tales of the elves of the forest. Then his
community came into contact with the wood elves of
Sylvanhome. When the idea of exchanging
"ambassadors" between the two communities came
up during the testy initial negotiations between
them, Fairley volunteered to live among the elves
and he stubbornly wore down his parents' objections
to the arrangement. Since then, he has lived in this
tree, while Ilwen Sylla's brother Caerwen went to live
with the humans (see location #4).

Fairley spends his days doing... well, not doing much
of anything that has even a touch of urgency to it. He
tries to learn as much as he can about the elves —
their culture, their mores, their history. But his
education has no end of term, no final examination.

No one — not his hosts, nor the community that he
left behind — has thought about what will become of
him in another half-year, or year, or even ten years.
To make his situation more awkward, not everyone in

Sylvanhome wants to humor him, and some won't even give him the time of day.

As a consequence, he keeps company with the retired elder, Elna Longsea (see location #12). They both have a lot of idle time, and Sylvanhome has no one better to teach Fairley about the elves (except perhaps Lucan the bard, who has no interest in doing any such thing).

On the whole, Fairley feels safe in Sylvanhome. His only possession that can pass for a weapon is a utility knife (treat it as a dagger), but he carries it with him at all times. Apart from occasional anxiety about his long-term future here, he has no real worries even though he knows that not everyone likes having a human in their midst. However, he did have a mild scare when he fell asleep the shade of a tree one afternoon. This drew a crowd, as the elves, who do not sleep as humans do, had no idea what to make of him. Finally, someone poked him to see if he was dead. Fairley then woke up out of a deep sleep to find a crowd of elves standing over him and peering at him with intense curiosity.

Treasure: Fairley has little in the way of valuables. He wears a turquoise pendant on a thin electrum chain around his neck; it's worth 20 gp at most. Before he left for Sylvanhome, his family gave him a purse with 100 sp in it for living expenses. He still has all of it because the elves feed him for free.

9. Aela and Luven Welleaf's Workshop

This spacious house doubles as a workshop and the family home of Aela and Luven Welleaf and their two children. The largest room houses a loom on which Aela spins spider webs into silk. From that silk she makes rope that is both exceptionally light and durable. Her rope weighs only 5 pounds per length of 50 feet, has AC 18, and each length has 10 hit points.

Aela refuses to sell or barter for her rope (so does everyone else in the family, if approached). Instead, she refers all interested parties to her uncle Lio Welleaf (see location #7), the village merchant. Lio's store is their sole distributor. These Welleafs consider themselves artisans and they have no interest in running a business.

Luven's job is gathering raw materials for his wife. He focuses on abandoned webs; usually, there is little point in messing with spiders in their lair. But Luven recently found an enormous web that looked to good to pass up because the fibers were so strong and thick. Unfortunately, the web was still occupied by proportionately large and aggressive spiders. Much to his wife's annoyance, Luven won't stop talking about what a haul this web would provide, if only those damned spiders weren't in the way. Much to her alarm, he also talks about bringing their young children with him to help clear them out.

If the party strikes up a conversation with Aela and Luven, Aela perks up when she realizes that they are adventurers:

Aela turns to her husband and says, "Luven, they're adventurers! They can help you with that spider web you were talking about."

"What, that?" Luven turns to you and explains: "I found this huge web in the forest. Beautiful silk, very strong. Aela would do wonders with it. But the spiders — big spiders. I wanted to harvest that web right then and there but it was just me versus them and well, you know...."

"So let's hire these people to take care of them. If those spiders are so large, they could become a menace. What if they attacked someone?"

"We don't need to hire anyone. I'll take the children with me."

"You'll do no such thing."

Aela promises the party a reward if they agree to clear out the spiders. If the party agrees, Luven takes them to a spot out in the forest and shows them a vast spider web about 20 feet long and 10 feet tall anchored on either side by the trunk of a tree. It's guarded by two giant spiders who don't like having their base of operations harvested for rope-making material.

Defeating the spiders allows Luven to harvest the web. Upon their return, Aela gives the party 100 sp and tells them to come back in several days. At that time, she presents them with a 50-foot length of her spider silk rope.

Treasure: Aela and Luven don't have much coin handy considering the value of her handiwork; they barter with Lio for most of what they need. They keep 20 gp and 500 sp in a sack in their bedroom.

10. Uwel the Scout

Sylvanhome has always considered itself a safe place nestled deep in the forest. The elves feel comfortable here. But that feeling of safety relies on knowing what is happening beyond the guard posts, and the forest of trees blocks their sight lines as it does for everyone else. That is where Uwel Elbrand comes in.

Uwel serves the village as its full-time scout. He succeeded Ilwen Sylla in that role when she became garrison commander several years ago. He is impulsive by nature and too young to have learned the value of caution, and as a rogue he relies on his talent for stealth and evasion to do his job more than on woodcraft and savvy. Both Guillen Longesea and Ilwen admire Uwel's daring, but they worry that someday he's going to get himself into trouble from which they cannot rescue him.

This modest house near the edge of the village serves Uwel as his home and base of operations. As darkness falls, he rappels down on a spider silk rope and scampers off into the forest, constantly alert to signs of unusual activity. He returns at dawn and reports to Ilwen if he has found anything out of the ordinary. Therefore, he can only be found here during the day.

Treat Uwel as a 1st level rogue (see NPC stat blocks).

Treasure: Uwel wears around his neck a small silver talisman in the shape of the elven deity's holy symbol with his name engraved on the back on a steel chain. It's worth 10 gp, based mostly on its workmanship. He also keeps a gold ring with a ruby set it in it, worth 1,000 gp, hidden under some clothes tossed onto the floor. Otherwise, his personal wealth amounts to little more than items that he has scavenged in the course of his duties. They lie scattered around his house. 80 sp, 98 cp, a light crossbow with a cracked stock and 12 bolts are the only items of note; however one of the bolt is magical — a *+1 bolt*. Uwel will not miss any of this stuff if it goes missing, not even the magic bolt.

11. Darail Family

The Darail family lives on the outskirts of the village. If the party finds itself near their house, they see the parents, Ilias and Lidia Darail, outside the house in a state of distress. If the party engages them in conversation:

"Our son is missing!" Lidia exclaims.

Ilias says, "Aden always goes into the forest to play, but he never wanders far. But when we called for him to come in, he was nowhere to be found."

"Do you think the humans could have taken him?" Lidia says. "Lucan is always saying that they mean to do us harm."

If the party agrees to help find Aden, his parents take them into the forest just beyond their house, where the boy is wont to play. There is no obvious physical evidence to be found, except that a successful DC 10 Wisdom (Perception) or Wisdom (Survival) check reveals a fresh set of footprints small enough to have been made by an elven child leading off into the forest.

If the party follows it, they quickly find that it leads them to a dead tree with a hollow trunk. A pack of six wolves has fixated on the tree; they growl menacingly as they crouch before a hole in the trunk that is just too small for any one of them to get through it. Defeating the wolves allows the party to discover an elven boy huddled in the hollow trunk, shaken but unharmed. If asked, Aden Darail explains that he chased after a squirrel while playing near his house, and before he knew it the wolves set upon him.

Aden's parents are ecstatic at his safe return, of course. They offer the party all of their household wealth at the moment — 200 sp and a semi-precious gem worth 50 gp — as a reward. The party also gains a +2 bonus to all Charisma-based skill tests involving a resident of Sylvanhome from this point forward, as word of their heroism spreads through the village.

If the party refuses to help, Aden's parents turn to Guillen Longsea (see location #3) for help, who in turn tasks Ilwen Sylla (see location #4) and Uwel the scout (see location #10) with finding him. However, they cannot locate the boy and his disappearance remains unsolved. After a while, the party (especially its human members) notice villagers giving them distrustful looks.

Treasure: As mentioned above, the Darail family have no coin or other such valuables other than what they offer to the party as a reward for rescuing Aden. However, the family does have a longbow of exceptional quality (a family heirloom) as its militia weapon. Treat it as a non-magical *+1 longbow*.

Scaling the Encounter: If average level of the party is 4 or higher use dire wolves instead of wolves.

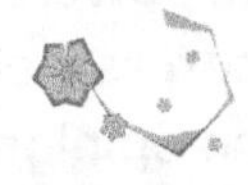

12. Elna Longsea's Retreat

Even by elven standards, Elna Longsea has reached a venerable age. She has lived long enough to weary of leadership and its burdens, and years ago she retired and left the position of village elder to her son, Guillen (see location #3). Since then, she has lived in this small house at the edge of the village and devoted herself to contemplation and communing with the deity of the elves.

The villagers still revere her and refer to her as the Lady Elna, but since her retirement she has refused to involve herself in Sylvanhome's affairs. She is willing to use her divine powers on their behalf, but out of respect for her son as well as genuine weariness, she offers no opinions on matters of public importance. If the party comes to her, she agrees to heal them, cure them, or otherwise use her divine spell casting to help them, as long as it is within her power and no harm to Sylvanhome will come of it. However, if the party asks her to intervene in village affairs, she refuses.

It should be noted that Elna has befriended the human Fairley Rehn (see location #8) since his arrival as a hostage. She did not do this deliberately, but the lad wanted to learn about the history and ways of the elves and oddly enough, the one thing that she shared with him was that neither of them had anything better to do. This has had a subtle effect on Elna's mindset. Without being fully aware of it, her friendship with Fairley has made her more accepting of humans than she had ever been when she was elder, when she knew of them only as an abstraction.

Treat Elna Longsea as a 5th level cleric (see NPC stat blocks).

Treasure: Elna Longsea has no personal wealth except for a couple of heirlooms that she took with her into retirement: a tiara wrought from fine platinum strands worth 500 gp and a gold pendant inlaid with an emerald worth 350 gp.

13. Arn the Gnome's Camp

There is a small tent pitched just outside the village periphery. It is small because it belongs to a gnome named Arn. Arn is a traveling salesman. He'll sell almost anything, but at the moment he represents a team of craftsmen in a city not too far distant who make crossbows of exceptional quality.

He came to Sylvanhome convinced of his ability to sell anything to anyone. Taking a shortcut through the forest on his way to the next town, he noticed the sentries (see location #1) drawing their trademark elven longbows. He figured that he could talk the elves of Sylvanhome into ditching them for his crossbows, knowing that crossbows — especially the crossbows he has with him — gain in stopping power what they give up in range compared to longbows. After all, how much long-distance shooting happens in a thick forest?

However, he could not persuade Ilwen Sylla or anyone else in Sylvanhome. In fact, only their good manners prevented them from giving him the bum's rush. No matter what trick of the salesman's trade he employed, he made no apparent impression on them. After telling the party his tale, he sighs and

declares that he'll sleep on it tonight, and if he can't
think of a different sales pitch, he'll cut his losses and
move on.

If the party let it slip that they're going on a mission
with Ilwen (see Chapter 4), Arn perks up.

> "Hold on, now," Arn says. "Those elves won't listen
> to me. But maybe they'll listen to you. Eh? Sounds
> like they trust you if they'll take you into the
> woods with them."
>
> He takes a crossbow from the sacks on his little
> cart and hands it to you. "Take it," he says. "A
> demonstration model, if you get my meaning. Talk
> it up to the elves, kill a couple of forest monsters
> with it to show 'em what it can do. And if you can
> close the sale, I'll split my profit with you even-up
> for both of us. That won't leave me with a lot, but
> that don't matter — it's about a salesman's pride
> now. What about it?"

If they party accepts Arn's proposal, they get a free
crossbow. Arn's crossbows are just about as good as
advertised; they are not magical but their
craftsmanship makes them exceptionally accurate
and they grant a +1 bonus to attack rolls made with

them. However, the party stands no chance of persuading the elves to give up their longbows for Arn's crossbows. They refuse politely, but quite firmly.

Treasure: Arn carries on his belt a pouch, into which he dips to cover expenses and the occasional bribe. At the moment, he has 85 gp on him. More significantly, he pulls behind him wherever he goes a small cart with 12 of his high-quality heavy crossbows, for which his asking price is 100 gp each.

14. Bandit Encampment

A band of nine human bandits has improvised a base of operations in and beneath this abandoned treehouse. However, only the bandit leader uses the house for shelter — rank has its privileges. Her followers sleep on the ground under the tree.

The nature of their business is such so that the bandits don't know how long they'll stay here, but their presence complicates matters for both the elves of Sylvanhome and the more lawful humans who share the forest with them. They don't much care whom they prey upon, although other humans are profitable targets because the elves don't seem to carry coin. But many of the wood elves who live in Sylvanhome don't care to distinguish between good humans and bad humans, or they are too innocent of the wider world to know enough to do so.

Treat the bandit leader as a bandit captain and her followers as bandits. For guidance on scaling them up, see Chapter 3.

Treasure: All of the gang's booty is kept in the treehouse under the leader's jealous guard. It consists of 300 gp and 2,010 sp in sacks and loose piles.

Chapter 2: Lucan's Cunning

If the party successfully fetched the greenstone fruit for Lucan (see location #5), he may trust them with a devious and much more consequential mission. If you wish to use this chapter, invent some pretext for the party encountering Lucan. If the bard has resolved to set this plan in motion, he has also resolved to find the party to carry it out for him. So at that point, he is looking for them.

> The bard's countenance brightens at the sight of you. "Ah! How fortunate to find you here." He bows with a practiced flourish. "May the sun smile upon you, my friends. Have you a moment? There is an urgent matter that I wish to share with you."
>
> Lucan shepherds you to a quiet spot, confident that no one will overhear. He continues: "Listen. You have proven to me that you are friends of Sylvanhome, and you are the only ones I can trust at this dire hour. I have reliable information that the life of our own Caerwen Sylla is in grave danger — the humans wish to kill him and set off a war with Sylvanhome!

"We must not let this happen! I have warned his sister, and I have warned Guillen, but both of them are so blind to the humans and their schemes that they will not listen. You are the only ones I can trust! Do this for Sylvanhome, and I will reward you handsomely."

Lucan proceeds to tell the party that Caerwen's daily routine involves a constitutional in which he walks out to a certain tree about a half-mile from the hunters' camp (under escort, of course) and then back. Lucan claims that today, Caerwen's guards will kill him when they reach that tree. He instructs the party to rescue Caerwen from his would his would-be assassins and take him to a safe house — an abandoned house outside the village that Lucan owns — and keep him there for one week, after which they may return to Sylvanhome.

If the party mentions consulting with Ilwen Sylla or Guillen Longsea (or Elna Longsea, for that matter), Lucan urges them not to do so — there is no time! If the party presses Lucan, he insists that he has spies within the hunters' camp. This is a lie, but his information about Caerwen's routine is accurate.

If the party agrees to carry out Lucan's mission, they

find Caerwen and an escort of two hunters at the spot that Lucan described. The guards show no sign of tension or impending action. If the party attacks, Caerwen will try to flee back to the hunters' camp and if the party tries to grapple him, he resists.

Of course, Lucan knows that kidnapping Caerwen Sylla will set off a diplomatic crisis. If the party executes Lucan's plan and spirits away Caerwen, the hunters send an angry delegation to Sylvanhome demanding his return, or the return of their own hostage, Fairley Rehn (see location #8) and satisfaction for whatever the party did to Caerwen's escort. Elder Guillen Longsea cannot find Caerwen as long as the party has him in custody, but neither does the elder have the gumption to keep them from taking Fairley back with them.

When the party brings Caerwen back to Sylvanhome after the interval that Lucan specified, they find that everything that transpired in their absence is a done deal. Both former hostages are safe, and in one sense nothing worse has happened than the return of the *status quo ante*. Undoing their exchange breaks the bonds of trust that it created. Repairing them will take much effort, if it is possible at all.

For their efforts, Lucan gives the party 200 gp.

Chapter 3:
Uwel Among the Bandits

If the party has not yet discovered that Uwel the scout is hiding a valuable ring in his house (see location #10), give the party the opportunity to hear (or overhear) gossip that he was recently seen flaunting a gold ring with a beautiful ruby set in it. He refused to say where he got it, but nobody can recall seeing him with anything so valuable ever before. A gathering in the Speaker's Clearing (see location #2) fueled by Lucan's distilled beverages would make a suitable occasion. Fairley Rehn, who observes and hears everything, is another possible source of loose talk.

Then, while the party is out in the forest they see on the ground a silver talisman in the shape of the elven deity's holy symbol. If the party has already met Uwel in person, they automatically recognize it as his (see location #10). If not, close inspection reveals to anyone who can read elven runes that his name is engraved on the back. If you wish, use this in place of the "Uwel at work" encounter described in Table 1.1.

Uwel himself is nowhere in sight. However, a

successful DC 8 Wisdom (Perception) or Wisdom
(Survival) check reveals several sets of tracks leading
off into the forest. One set of tracks is clearly not
footprints; they were made by boot heels dragged
along the ground.

Following them leads to the bandit encampment at
location #14. Once the clearing comes into view, the
party sees Uwel hanging upside down from a low
branch, stripped to the waist and his feet bound
together by a rope. Several of the bandits have clubs
and they take turns beating his unclothed upper
body.

The bandit leader, a tall, wiry woman, stands off to
one side. She shoulders aside her followers to
approach Uwel. A wolfish grin creases her face as
she leans down to get nose-to-nose with him.

"My, what a handsome little elf boy we have here.
Now: Tell me what you did with that ring that you
stole from us, won't you?" Uwel wriggles and
gasps, but says nothing intelligible. The smile
disappears from the bandit leader's face. She
turns to her followers. "Keep at it until he talks,"
she says, then walks away.

Uwel did steal the ring, of course. During one of his scouting missions, he couldn't restrain himself from sneaking into the bandit encampment and making off with the most valuable item he could find. The bandits suspected the local elves, and when they found Uwel at his work, they surrounded him and hauled him off.

The bandits keep beating Uwel — and eventually, they will kill him — until the party intervenes.

If the party rescues Uwel — whether by force or persuasion — he thanks them profusely and the party's standing in Sylvanhome rises. However, as the news of what happened to him spreads through the village, the fact that he was kidnapped and tortured by humans cannot be denied and a subtle current of anti-human sentiment flows under the celebration over Uwel's rescue.

If they allow the bandits to torture Uwel to death — and he will die before he admits to stealing the ring — then the bandits eventually attack Sylvanhome and ransack as many homes as they can until they are either driven off or they find the ring.

Treasure: If the party defeats the bandits, they find the treasure described in location #14.

Scaling the Encounter: Treat the leader as a bandit captain and her followers as bandits. If you want to make a fight with the gang more challenging, treat the leader as a veteran and her followers as thugs.

Chapter 4: Night Patrol

The party receives one more chance to intervene in Sylvanhome's affairs if they meet at least one of these preconditions:

- They helped Luvan Welleaf clear out the spider web (see location #9).
- They rescued Aden Darail from the wolves (see location #11).
- They rescued Uwel the scout from the bandits (see Chapter 3).

If any of the above apply, the party spots Ilwen Sylla passing under one of the guard posts as she returns to the village. She seems distracted, her face creased with thought. But she comes to when she sees the party.

> "Ah! You're still here," she says. She pauses, examining all of you closely, as if considering what she is about to say. "Hear me, outlanders. In my eyes, you have proven yourselves friends of Sylvanhome, so I trust you. I may have need of

your help.

"I have just met with one of the leaders of the humans. He said that one of his people died this morning. He went into the forest by himself during the night, and when he came back he was… transformed. A wolf-man set upon him and bit him. He was already growing fur and fangs, and his eyes looked unlike a man's eyes. He bade his fellows take their silvered sword and slay him before he slew them. So they did."

Ilwen flinches at the thought. Then she continues: "The leader, named Edgar, proposed that he and I should each take some of our people and patrol the forest together tonight. If there are wolf-men near here, they threaten elves and humans in equal measure.

"I cannot speak for Edgar. But I would rather not take any of our folk on such an errand. They have no experience of actual fighting, nor do they have the weapons to take on a were-creature. Guillen and the Lady Elna are too valuable to risk; if either of them were lost, the hearts of our folk would falter. But you — you are stout heroes. Will you go with me tonight and help me stand for Sylvanhome?"

If the party agrees, Ilwen tells them to meet her at location #2 when the moon rises. She has ten arrows with heads that Lin the fletcher (see location #6) has fashioned from silver coins. Treat them as silvered arrows, but not Lin's trademark mundane *+1 arrows*. Ilwen keeps four for herself and gives the rest to the party. From her headquarters, she leads them to the designated rendezvous point out in the forest. In the light of the full moon, they find five humans carrying longbows waiting for them. A tall, rangy man with shaggy hair steps forward and holds his palms outward.

"Hail and well met, Ilwen Sylla," he says.

Ilwen returns the gesture. "May the moon smile upon you, Edgar."

A wry smile creases one side of Edgar's face. "We've a good moon for hunting werewolves, to be sure," he says. "I brought four of our best hunters with me." Then he examines each party member with a querying look. "And you brought... elves?"

"They are friends of Sylvanhome," Ilwen replies. "I tell you honestly: As I left our meeting today, I doubted that anyone from my garrison would stand against a were-beast. These friends are adventurers. They are used to hazards."

"But our deal was that our communities would share the risk of this mission. We would work alongside your elves."

"Edgar, as skilled as we elves are with a bow — this is a danger of a higher order. If I did not bring the strongest fighters I could find, it would put your people at greater risk. What kind of diplomacy would that be?"

Edgar ponders her words. He turns to his followers, who shrug. One of his hunters calls out, "We're here to kill a wolf-man, Edgar."

Edgar chuckles. Then he says to Ilwen, "That was well said. Let's go."

With that, everyone heads off into the deep forest toward the area where Edgar believes his unfortunate comrade was attacked. The moon is bright enough so that the humans can see fairly well without torches. They fan out on either side behind Edgar, but stay close by.

After an hour of carefully picking their way through the trees in the dim light, the group comes upon a small clearing and sees two large humanoids spotted with patches of thick fur, looking up at the moon and howling.

Unless the party achieves surprise, the werewolves turn on the group and immediately attack. The werewolves begin the encounter in their hybrid form. Ilwen and the humans all try to keep their distance so that they can fire their silver-tipped arrows without hindrance, as they have no other weapon that can harm it.

Treat Edgar as a 2nd level ranger (see NPC stat blocks) equipped with a silvered longsword and his followers as scouts, each equipped with two silvered arrows.

Treasure: The werewolves have no treasure on them.

Scaling the Encounter: Even with the NPC reinforcements, two werewolves may prove a substantial challenge for a low-level party. Ilwen and the hunters all have silvered arrows, but they will run out of them quickly enough. If the werewolves are not down by then, they will keep firing mundane arrows at the lycanthropes to distract them, but they can't do any more damage at that point.

If the average party level is 1-3, feel free to have one of the werewolves flee as soon as the other is killed, or to have both flee when they are reduced to less than half of their hit points but killing both would be glorious, of course, don't feel obligated to allow bad luck to allow the werewolves to crush the party and their allies.

If the average party level is higher than 6, consider throwing in a third werewolf to make the encounter more challenging.

Conclusion:

Of course, the party is free to depart Sylvanhome without engaging in anything described in Chapters 2-4. They leave the village as they found it, still uncertain about the future and the nature and intentions of their new human neighbors. Allowing the bandits at location #14 to continue as they are muddies the waters, as they are bound to grow bolder and attack elves who venture into the forest. A substantial number of elves, egged on by Lucan the bard, will fail to distinguish (or simply refuse to distinguish) between the bad humans who rob and kill them and the benign humans who are willing at heart to hunt and forage in the forest as peaceful neighbors.

However, if they choose to stick around Sylvanhome for a bit and engage in any or all of Chapters 2-4, a variety of outcomes are possible.

If the party kidnaps Caerwen Sylla and completes Lucan's mission in Chapter 2, they return to find Sylvanhome tense, but stable for the moment. Returning each hostage to his native community preserves equilibrium, but hardens feelings on both sides. Both the party and the elves of Sylvanhome find that encounters with the hunters are less friendly than in the past. The danger exists that hotheads in the human camp will organize an attack on Sylvanhome, especially if the party harmed Caerwen's guards in freeing him.

It is also possible that tensions will build within Sylvanhome, as the arguments between the factions led by Lucan and Ilwen become more heated. Guillen Longsea remains timid and indecisive, so he lets the situation fester. Civil war within Sylvanhome becomes a possibility.

No matter what happens, over time the party finds that Sylvanhome treats them with deeper suspicion and more obvious hostility. Even less welcome here than before, they may find it wisest to leave.

On the other hand, if the party refuses to carry out Lucan's mission, the situation remains as it was when they first arrived, except that the bard becomes their enemy. Once they refuse him, Lucan sees them as bad outsiders (as opposed to outsiders whom he can manipulate) but he does not act against them in the short term. If the party stays in Sylvanhome for a long period of time, he works on plans to get rid of them.

Another possibility is that even though the party created a bad situation by doing Lucan's bidding in

Chapter 2, Chapter 3 presents them with a chance to repair at least some of the damage. Rescuing Uwel raises the villagers' estimation of the party and makes their stay in Sylvanhome more comfortable.

If it gets out that Uwel stole the ring from the bandits, Guillen Longsea and Ilwen Sylla both roll their eyes, as one would show exasperation at a misbehaving child. He took something that did not belong to the elves. But on the other hand, if there is anyone left from the bandit gang, it hardly seems appropriate to give it back to them. Ilwen confiscates the ring from Uwel and suggests to Guillen that he offer it to the hunters as a goodwill gift.

Rescuing Uwel to close out Chapter 3 certainly lays the groundwork for Chapter 4 in that it convinces Ilwen to trust the party (that is, if she had any doubts before).

Once the group defeats the werewolves, Ilwen and Edgar look at each other and smile in relief.

> "Well... It's over," Edgar says.
>
> "Your hunters showed great courage. I salute you, and them," Ilwen says.

Edgar grins as he catches his breath. "And you, Ilwen Sylla — you fight to win. I respect that. I guess I always knew elves were smart."

The two of them shake hands.

If anyone in the group has been afflicted with lycanthropy from the battle, Ilwen suggests that they return to Sylvanhome right away and have Elna Longsea cast *remove curse*. The hunters are particularly grateful for this suggestion, as they would otherwise feel the need to kill the afflicted party before he becomes a menace (as happened with their unfortunate comrade). This creates a dramatic scene as they rush back to the elven village and Ilwen barks at the sentry to stand down and let them pass. But all ends well, with humans impressed and grateful at Elna's willingness to help.

Sharing a successful experience of battle improves relations between the elves and the humans. It gives them a common touchstone that they can both celebrate. From this point onward, it becomes much less likely that random encounters in the forest between elves and humans will result in conflict, as both communities regard the other more favorably. Formal meetings between Sylvanhome and the hunters become more common, with Ilwen and

Edgar taking the lead. It is still too early to speak of them as allies, but long-term peace between the two communities now seems more likely than short-term conflict.

The party's deeds during their sojourn in Sylvanhome played an important role in shaping a hopeful vision of the future. Elves have long memories as well as long lives, so the player characters will always find a friendly welcome — no more arrows aimed at their chests — in this corner of the forest.

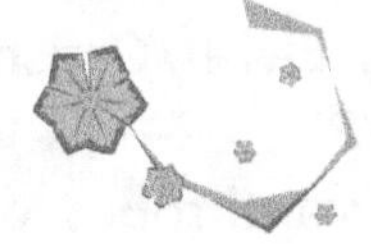

NPC's and Creatures

Stat blocks for all other NPC's can be found in the *Dungeons & Dragons Monster Manual.*

Edgar

2nd Level Ranger
Medium human, neutral good
Armor Class 13 (14 with leather armor)
Hit Points 20 (2d10+4)
Speed 30 ft.
STR 13 (+1) DEX 16 (+3) CON 14 (+2) INT 10 (0) WIS 15 (+2) CHA 12 (+1)

Saving Throws Strength +3, Dexterity +5
Skills Insight +4, Nature +2, Survival +4
Senses Passive Perception 12
Languages Common, Elvish, Orcish
Challenge: 1/4 (50 XP)
Favored Enemies: Lycanthropes, orcs.
Spellcasting. Edgar is a 2nd-level spellcaster. Spell save DC 12, +4 to hit with spell attacks.

1st level: *animal friendship, cure wounds*

<u>Actions</u>
Longsword. Melee Weapon Attack. +3 to hit, reach 5 ft., one target. *Hit:* 1d8+1 slashing damage.
Longbow. Ranged Weapon Attack. +6 to hit, range 150/600 ft., one target. Hit: 1d8+1 piercing damage.

Elna Longsea

5th Level Cleric
Medium elf, chaotic good
Armor Class 11
Hit Points 33 (5d8+5)
Speed 30 ft.
STR 10 (0) DEX 12 (+1) CON 12 (+1) INT 15 (+2) WIS 16 (+3) CHA 17 (+3)

Saving Throws Wisdom +6, Charisma +6
Skills History +5, Religion +5
Senses Passive Perception 13
Languages Common, Elvish
Challenge: 1/2 (100 XP)

Spellcasting. Elena Longs is a 5th-level spellcaster.
Spell save DC 14, +6 to hit with spell attacks.

Cantrips: *guidance, sacred flame, spare the dying*
1st level: *bless, create water, cure wound, protection from evil, sanctuary, shield of faith*
2nd level: *aid, lesser restoration, protection from poison, spiritual weapon*
3rd level: *remove curse, magic circle*

Actions
Longbow. Ranged Weapon Attack. +1 to hit, range 150/600 ft., one target. Hit: 1d8 piercing damage.

Guillen Longsea

2nd Level Cleric
Medium elf, neutral good
Armor Class 11
Hit Points 17 (1d8+4)
Speed 30 ft.
STR 12 (+1) DEX 13 (+1) CON 15 (+2) INT 14 (+2) WIS 15 (+2) CHA 12 (+1)

Saving Throws Wisdom +4, Charisma +3
Skills History +4, Religion +4
Senses Passive Perception 12
Languages Common, Elvish
Challenge: 1/4 (50 XP)

Spellcasting. Guile Longsea is a 2nd-level spellcaster. Spell save DC 12, +4 to hit with spell attacks.

Cantrips: *guidance, sacred flame, spare the dying*
1st level: *bless, create water, cure wound, protection from evil, sanctuary, shield of faith*

<u>Actions</u>
Longbow. Ranged Weapon Attack. +1 to hit, range 150/600 ft., one target. Hit: 1d8+1 piercing damage.

Ilwen Sylla

3rd Level Ranger
Medium elf, neutral good
Armor Class 13 (15 with leather armor)
Hit Points 26 (3d10+6)
Speed 30 ft.
STR 12 (+1) DEX 16 (+3) CON 14 (+2) INT 11 (0) WIS 15 (+2) CHA 10 (0)

Saving Throws Strength +3, Dexterity +5
Skills Acrobatics +5, Investigation +4, Survival +4
Senses Passive Perception 12
Languages Elvish, Common
Challenge: 1/2 (100 XP)

Spellcasting. Ilwen Sylla is a 3rd-level spellcaster.
Spell save DC 12, +4 to hit with spell attacks.

1st level: *cure wounds, hail of thorns, hunter's mark*

<u>Actions</u>
Longsword. *Melee Weapon Attack.* +3 to hit, reach 5 ft., one
target. *Hit:* 1d8+1 slashing damage.
Longbow. *Ranged Weapon Attack.* +5 to hit, range 150/600 ft.,
one target. Hit: 1d8+1 piercing damage.

Lucan Bellfae

5th Level Bard
Medium elf, chaotic neutral
Armor Class 12
Hit Points 33 (5d8+5)
Speed 30 ft.
STR 11 (0) DEX 15 (+2) CON 13 (+1) INT 16 (+3) WIS 15 (+2) CHA 18 (+4)

Saving Throws Dexterity +5, Charisma +7
Skills Athletics +2, Deception +7, History +6, Insight +5, Intimidation +7, Performance +10
Senses Passive Perception 12
Languages Common, Elvish
Challenge: 1 (200 XP)

Spellcasting. Lucan Bellfae is a 5th-level spellcaster. Spell save DC 15, +7 to hit with spell attacks.

Cantrips: *dancing lights, minor illusion, vicious mockery*
1st level: *charm person, detect magic, comprehend languages, faerie fire*
2nd level: *enthrall, invisibility*
3rd level: *dispel magic, fear*

Actions

Shortsword. *Melee Weapon Attack.* +3 to hit, reach 5 ft., one target. Hit: 1d6 piercing damage.
Longbow. *Ranged Weapon Attack.* +4 to hit, range 150/600 ft., one target. Hit: 1d8 piercing damage.

Ranger Smith

1st Level Ranger
Medium human, lawful neutral
Armor Class 10 (12 with hide armor)
Hit Points 10 (1d10)
Speed 30 ft.
STR 10 (0) DEX 10 (0) CON 10 (0) INT 10 (0) WIS 10 (0) CHA 10 (0)

Saving Throws Strength +2, Dexterity +2
Skills Investigation +2, Nature +2, Survival +2
Senses Passive Perception 10
Languages Common, Elvish
Challenge: 1/8 (25 XP)

Actions
Longbow. *Ranged Weapon Attack.* +2 to hit, range 150/600 ft., one target. Hit: 1d8 piercing damage.

Uwel Elbrand

1st Level Rogue
Medium elf, chaotic good
Armor Class 14 (15 with hide armor)
Hit Points 9 (1d8+1)
Speed 30 ft.
STR 10 (0) DEX 18 (+4) CON 13 (+1) INT 10 (0) WIS 9 (-1) CHA 16 (+3)

Saving Throws Dexterity +6, Intelligence +2
Skills Acrobatics +6, Deception +5, Sleight of Hand +6, Stealth +6
Senses Passive Perception 9
Languages Common, Elvish
Challenge: 1/2 (100 XP)

Sneak Attack (1/Turn). Uwel Elbrand deals an 1d6 extra damage when he hits a target with a weapon attack and has advantage on the attack roll, or when the target is within 5 feet of an ally of his that isn't incapacitated and he doesn't have disadvantage on the attack roll.

<u>Actions</u>
Shortsword. *Melee Weapon Attack.* +2 to hit, reach 5 ft., one target. *Hit:* 1d6 piercing damage.
Longbow. *Ranged Weapon Attack.* +4 to hit, range 150/600 ft., one target. Hit: 1d8 piercing damage.

NEW MAGIC ITEM: Idol of Sylvanhome
Wondrous item, artifact

The *Idol of Sylvanhome* is a devotional item that belongs to the wood elf village of Sylvanhome. It is a 4-foot tall statue carved from dense hardwood in a representation of the holy symbol of the deity of the elves. It has no decoration — no inlaid gems or precious metals. Its origin is mysterious; not even Lucan the bard knows all of its history.

The idol does not serve just anyone. It is permanently attuned to the current village elder of Sylvanhome. Whenever a new elder is formally appointed, the former elder, if still alive, automatically loses his or her connection to the artifact and the successor becomes attuned to it. No one else may use the idol's power.

Healing Word: Once every eight hours, the elder of Sylvanhome may activate the idol. The benign will of the elven deity flows through the elder, into the idol and manifests as healing energy. A number of targets equal to the elder's Wisdom bonus are affected as if the elder had cast the spell *healing word*, regardless of whether he or she is a spellcaster capable of casting *healing word*.

Sylvanhome

14
1
10
1
1
13
3
8
5
4
2
6
9
7
1
11
1
12
1
= 20 yds
Presume the entire map area is heavily wooded.
Callouts denote locations of interest.

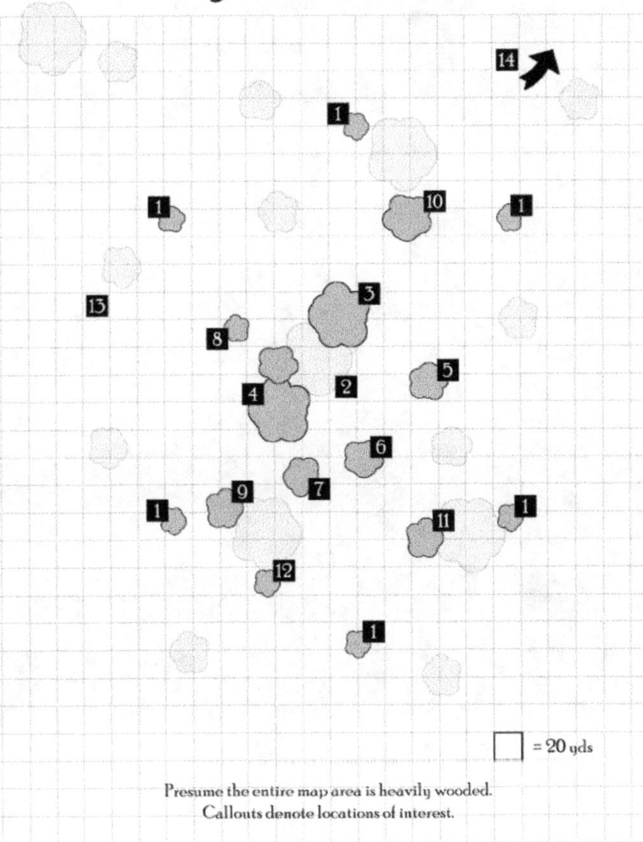

NOTES:

NOTES:

NOTES:

Module Design: Douglas Sun
Layout and Art Direction: Kimberly
Unger
Cover Art: Kimberly Unger

www.ingramcontent.com/pod-product-compliance
Lightning Source LLC
Chambersburg PA
CBHW070316120726
47910CB00007B/2507